The Collective Wisdom of

President Joe Biden

The Collective Wisdom of President Joe Biden

IBSN: 9798564085557

The Collective Wisdom of

President Joe Biden

"We hold these truths to be self-evident. All men and women created by the... go... you know... the thing!"

Benvolino Franklin